The Adventures of Me and Zee

The Old Oak Tree

MINA SHULER

outskirts press

Outskirts Press, Inc.
http://www.outskirtspress.com
ISBN: 978-1-9772-2353-1

Outskirts Press and the "OP" logo are trademarks belonging to Outskirts Press, Inc.

PRINTED IN THE UNITED STATES OF AMERICA

This Book Belongs to:

_____

Deep in the forest lived 2 young squirrels named Ty and Zee and every day they went on a new adventure. Sometimes the adventure seemed good and sometimes it was bad but they learned a lesson every time.

One afternoon Ty woke up and jumped out of bed looked and said, "There goes Zee waiting for me", he ran down the stairs and out the door time to have fun and explore.

Ty: Hey Zee ready to have fun today, I thought that we could finish the adventure we started yesterday.

Zee: I have something better we can do its fun I promise, come on its true

Ty followed Zee through the forest towards the old oak tree he started to get nervous because his mom told him that is someplace he does not need to be.

Zee: Come Ty hurry up follow me, where going to climb the old oak tree

Ty: I don't want to climb the tree, and you shouldn't go up there, you know Mr. Owl lives here.

Zee: The owl is asleep we will be fine come on hurry up before I leave you behind

Ty didn't want to climb the tree or get left behind in the forest where the Owl lives, so he followed Zee up the old oak tree.

Ty: Shhhh, Zee, you're being too loud you have to stop shouting

Zee: But I am Haaapppppyyyyyy, he yelled and proud

Ty stopped and said Zee please stop being so loud

Zee: The Owl is asleep I told you its daytime not night you know owls don't come out during the daylight.

The squirrels continued to climb more and more but half way up they can hear a loud snore. Ty wanted to go back but Zee just didn't want to listen he was singing very loud because he felt he was going to complete the greatest mission. Zee stopped singing and the snoring did too Ty was scared and wasn't sure what to do. Ty and Zee stopped in a halt, Ty whispered to Zee, see this is all your fault. The squirrels turned around to head down the tree but it was too late the owl was awake hiding in the shadow so the squirrels couldn't see. They ran as fast as they could but the owl flew out and they yelled, "This isn't good".

Ty: Come on Zee follow me I see a place where we can be safe from harm

Zee: I thought I could talk to him and get him to stop with my charm

Ty: Bad idea Zee just follow me we need to get a place where we can be safe

The squirrels ran into the prickly bush and just in time because the owl was not too far behind. The owl with anger said, "You got away today, come back over here tomorrow to play", and flew away.

The squirrels waited for the coast to be clear
then ran fast away, faster than a running deer.
They made it home so full of fright, they were
glad they got home before it turned night.

Zee: See you tomorrow Ty that's enough adventure for me, we can try another one tomorrow.

Ty: Okay an adventure that is picked by me Zee

The boys looked at each other and laughed so loud, even though they were scared they were happy they made it home safe and that made them proud. They knew they were in harm's way and will never do it again another day or will they.

The End

CPSIA information can be obtained at www.ICGtesting.com
Printed in the USA
LVIW010048090221
678786LV00010B/50